The Roaring

Dragon *of* Redrose

by Jan Slepian *and* Ann Seidler

illustrated by Richard E. Martin

Follett Publishing Company   Chicago

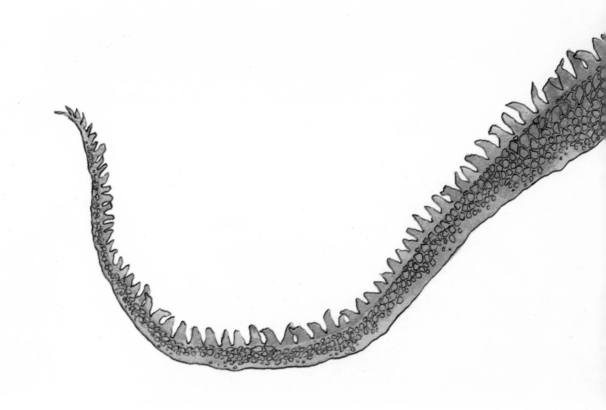

MANY years ago, in a faraway land, a dragon named Rodrigo lived all alone in a big cave near the friendly little town of Redrose. Rodrigo had no mother or father, no sisters or brothers—not even a close friend with whom he could pass the time. He was very lonely. He spent hours watching the happy, busy people of Redrose and wished with all his heart that he had a job in the town. Then he wouldn't be lonely. But what could he do, he wondered.

He was far too large to be a pet, led around on a leash like a dog. He couldn't give milk like a cow. And he knew his scales were far too sharp for people to ride on him comfortably. There just didn't seem to be any way for him to be useful so that he could live in Redrose.

8

One day as he was wistfully watching the townspeople come and go, he noticed they looked worried and unhappy. "Robbers! Robbers!" they shouted. "Help! Who can guard us from the robbers?"

"Oh, my goodness! Wobbers!" he said to himself. "If I were fwightening enough I could be the Town Pwotector. That's how I could be useful! Then I could belong to the town and never be lonely again."

He spent the rest of the day practicing at being frightening. He practiced blowing fire through his nose and ears. He practiced pointing his long forked tongue like a spear. He practiced jumping up and down to make the ground shake as it does in an earthquake. He snorted and stamped and made up a mighty roar, which he was sure would frighten even the boldest robbers.

"Now," he thought, "I am the most fwightening dwagon that ever was. The townspeople simply must ask me to be their Town Pwotector."

Early the next morning Rodrigo started up the fire in his ears and nose, stamped the ground to get a good start, and cleared his throat to get ready for his great roar.

He plunged out of his cave toward Redrose. When
the townspeople felt the ground shake and heard the noise,
they ran out of their houses to see what was happening.

13

"What is it? What can that awful noise be?" they cried. There at the town gate was Rodrigo. He lifted his fearful head and roared:

>Wace! Wun!
>
>Wobbers be done!
>
>The tewwible dwagon is here!

Not a sound was heard from the crowd.

He roared louder:

> Wace! Wun!
> Wobbers be done!
> The tewwible dwagon is here!

This time the little boy who was nearest the gate yawned, and people in the crowd began to whisper.
"Poor thing. Not a bit frightening."

"First robbers—now this!"

"Wonder who taught him dragoning!"

"Didn't you hear me?" asked poor Rodrigo. "I'm Wodwigo, a tewwible dwagon, weddy to pwotect you all fwom wobbers. Oh, I weally do want to stay and be your Town Pwotector."

"Town Protector!" shouted a man from the crowd. "Why, you can't roar right. 'Wace! Wun!' wouldn't frighten a mouse, let alone a robber."

"That's so," said another. "You're not right for the job."

Rodrigo hung his head and turned away sadly. He was about to return to his lonely cave.

Suddenly the little boy nearest the gate had a bright idea. He climbed to the top of the gate and said to the crowd, "Listen, everyone! It's not every town that can have a real, honest-to-goodness dragon. We *need* a Town Protector. We *need* to be safe from robbers."

"Wobbers!" the dragon repeated.

"Why don't we teach this dragon?" the boy went on. "See? He doesn't even know he isn't roaring right."

Rodrigo looked around hopefully. The townspeople talked together for a while.

"We would like to help—but how?" they asked.

"Mr. Dragon," said the little boy, "you have used your ears for fires much too long. Now you must use your ears for listening! Then you can learn to roar right."

"If I shake out the ashes I can listen to you all just fine . . . I think," said the dragon.

"We'll see," said the little boy, and he whispered to the crowd. "Shut your eyes, Mr. Dragon, shake out your ears, and *listen!*"

Rodrigo twitched his ears, tucked his long tail under him, and settled himself comfortably on the ground. He covered his eyes with a huge paw. It was plain to see that he was anxious to do his best.

Ding dong, ding dong, rang the town bell.

"Do you know what that is?" asked the boy.

"Uh . . . ah . . . let's see now . . . No. I give up!"

Scree . . . CLANK, clank! Some of the townspeople dropped the drawbridge over the moat.

"And that, Mr. Dragon?"

The dragon tapped his paw on the ground thoughtfully. "Don't tell me . . . mmm-mmm . . . Wobbers counting gold?"

Cr-r-r-reak, cr-reak. The rusty gate swung on its hinges.

"Gr-r-r-r, gr-r-r-r-r," a dog growled.

"R-r-r-r-r-r-r-r-r," the townspeople echoed.

"And those, Mr. Dragon? Those r-r-r sounds? Have you ever listened to any of those before?"

The ground began to tremble as the dragon's big hulk shook with laughter. "What funny, funny sounds! Oh dear! My old father used to sound like that when he was asleep.

"I must peek." He opened one huge eye and peered between his claws.

The boy sighed. "Oh, Mr. Dragon, it's plain to see you're just beyond help. You had better go home. There's no place for you here."

Rodrigo lumbered to his feet. There were large tears in his eyes. "Well, thanks anyway for the chance," he said softly.

"Maybe he's hungry after all his effort," called the vegetable man from his cart. "Here, have a bite," he said kindly, pushing his cart of ripe fruits and vegetables in front of Rodrigo. "Take your pick."

"Oh, thank you!" said Rodrigo politely. He really had been too nervous to eat breakfast, so that he was very hungry. He reached out for a ripe banana.

Just then the little boy had another idea. He clapped his hands gleefully and shouted, "Wait, Rodrigo! Let's not give up yet."

Rodrigo stopped, his neck outstretched and his mouth open.

"Maybe you were too hungry. You've got to hear the r-r-r sound in order to be able to roar. We'll get your hungry stomach to help your ears," the boy continued. "This is how we'll do it. You can eat your fill, but I will tell you *what* to eat. If you are hungry enough, your ears will have to work because you can eat only something that has the sound of r-r-r in it. Listen hard," he begged. "This is your last chance. Ready? We'll start with r-r-r-adishes."

"W-w . . . r-r-r-adishes?" Rodrigo thought. "Why, I *do* hear that r-r-r sound they have been telling me about!" And he hurriedly nibbled a dozen bunches of red radishes.

"Bananas," called out the boy.

The dragon looked at the bananas longingly, but shook his head. There was no r-r-r sound, and he wanted to be Town Protector even more than he wanted bananas.

"His ears really seem to be working," the townspeople murmured.

As the boy continued to call out the names of the fruits and vegetables, Rodrigo got to eat 60 car-r-r-ots and 10 bunches of gr-r-r-apes. He ate 87 or-r-r-anges, refused some lovely lettuce, but gulped down 38 gr-r-r-apefr-r-r-uit.

Soon he could eat no more. When the boy offered him some r-r-r-ed r-r-r-aspber-r-r-ies, Rodrigo gasped. "Oh, no! No wa . . . no *r-r-r*-aspber-*r-r*-ies, please. I w-w-w . . . *r-r-r*-eally couldn't eat another thing."

"*R-r-r*-aspber-*r-r*-ies! *R-r-r*-eally!" shouted the boy, throwing his cap into the air.

"His ears are really working!" cried the crowd. "It helped him get the roaring sound."

Rodrigo stared from one to another in disbelief.

"R-r-r-?" he tested. Then, "R-r-r-ace! R-r-r-un! R-R-R-OBBERS!" he roared triumphantly.

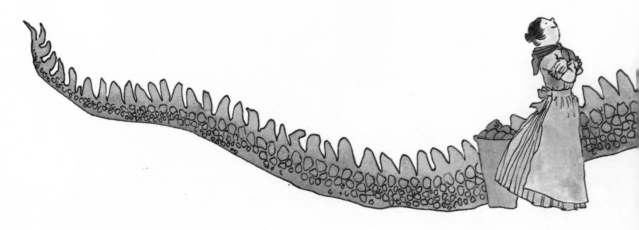

"Hurrah for the dragon! Hurrah for the boy!"
cheered the townspeople, as they joined hands and
danced around them.

That was how Rodrigo became the Town Protector, and
why he was never lonely again. Forever after, he kept
Redrose safe from robbers, for whenever danger approached
he raised his great head and roared his mighty roar:

> Race! Run!
> Robbers be done!
> The terrible dragon is here!

THE LISTEN-HEAR BOOKS

The Listen-Hear books provide teachers and parents with an entertaining and simple method of speech improvement for children in kindergarten and the early primary grades. The books also provide imaginative and enjoyable stories.

The books were written especially for the child who has an auditory discrimination problem and needs ear training but who has normal hearing and does not have a speech defect—the child who says *wed*, for instance, and thinks he is saying *red*. The stories and illustrations are so imaginative, however, that all children enjoy them. The stories also help all children develop good speaking habits, which in turn help develop good reading habits.

The books are ideal for read-aloud time. The *Teacher's Guide* for the set of six books provides instructions for games that the children can play after they have heard each story. The games give children practice in listening, hearing, and making the correct sounds.

Each book deals with one sound that many children find difficult to make:

> The Roaring Dragon of Redrose—for the sound of *R*
> Magic Arthur and the Giant—for the sound of *Th*
> Mr. Sipple and the Naughty Princess—for the sound of *S*
> The Cock Who Couldn't Crow—for the sound of *K*
> Alfie and the Dream Machine—for the sound of *F*
> Lester and the Sea Monster—for the sound of *L*

The authors, Jan Slepian and Ann Seidler, have each had more than ten years experience in speech therapy.

Mrs. Slepian has been a speech therapist at the Language Clinic at Massachusetts General Hospital in Boston and the National Hospital for Speech Disorders in New York.

Mrs. Seidler has been a speech therapist at the National Hospital for Speech Disorders in New York and speech consultant for the public schools of Cedar Grove, New Jersey.

Both authors are members of the American Speech and Hearing Association and the New Jersey Speech and Hearing Association.